THE TRAGEDY
OF

Belle Frank

THE TRAGEDY
OF
Belle Frank

Albert Cooper III

Dedication

I would like to dedicate this book to my family, The Cooper Family

I would like to thank my english teacher, Mr. O for inspiring me to continue my writing, and leading me where I'm at currently.

CHAPTER 1

The Unloved Student

Sophie Struss walks to her chemistry class, with earbuds ignoring the world around her. Closing the door behind her, she was greeted by the teacher sitting by the desk across the door.

"Late again, Sophie?" said Mr. Tus.

"Yeah" scoffed Sophie.

"Detention, after school...again." sighed Mr. Tus. "I know you are still sad about Belle's death but that's no excuse for being late again."

"Whatever," said Sophie

Taking her seat in the classroom, Sophie pulls out some papers which she starts working on instantly. Her concentration was suddenly interrupted when one of her earbuds was pulled out of her ear.

"What the f-" Sophie exclaimed.

"You still working on that?" said a fair-skinned boy.

"Yes, and stop pulling my earbuds damn it!"

"Hey!" yelled Mr. Tus. "Nolan that's detention for you too!"

"K.," said Nolan

"As for you Ms. Struss, I want to see you after class," said Mr. Tus

"Ooooo" said a random classmate.

"Shut up!" jeered Sophie.

As the school bell rang, the students emptied into the hallways leaving only Sophie and Mr. Tus inside the classroom.

"What is this about?" asked Sophie

"You know what this is about Ms. Struss," replied Mr. Tus

Sophie sighed in reply.

"Belle is dead Sophie, her death was ruled a suicide," said Mr. Tus

Sophie replied "That's not true, it doesn't make any sense for her to do that so I need to-

"Need to what? Find the person that supposedly killed her, the authorities already did an investigation and they didn't find anyone," said Mr. Tus

"That's why I need to find out myself," said Sophie

"She's dead!" yelled Mr. Tus. "It's been 6 months since her death, 3 months since the investigation was closed, so what makes you think that a high schooler can find what the professionals couldn't."

Sophie took a breath and said "I'm her best friend! I've been researching everyone she talked to before she died. So I believe that-

"Hand me the papers," said Mr. Tus.

"What? But this might be the only chance of finding her murderer?" replied Sohpie immediately.

"And if you think I'll let a sophomore get herself killed for a lost cause, then you're out of your mind. Now hand me the papers," said Mr. Tus sternly.

"But-" said Sophie.

"Don't make this any harder for you, either you can hand the papers right now and I'll let you off detention today or you could explain this to the principal." said, Mr. Tus.

"Fine!" cried out Sophie.

With tears forming in her eyes, she reached into her backpack and threw the papers at him. Leaving the classroom, she sprinted down the hallways into the female locker room where she sat in a corner and bitterly wept.

Meanwhile, while walking down the hallway to his next class, Nolan was stopped by one of his friends, a tall, dark-skinned athlete.

"What's up Jake?" asked Nolan.

"Dude, you missed it. I saw Sophie running to the locker room crying like a baby. Man, that was some comedy gold." said Jake.

"Come on' man, don't be a dick," said Nolan.

"Dude, besides you she literally has no friends. Well except for Belle but you know... yeah. Plus, all she ever talks about is finding her "killer", said Jake.

"Imma talk to her afterschool," said Nolan.

"Nah, someone told me your ass got detention for trying to flirt with her during class," said Jake.

"Mr. Tus was just being an ass cause his wife left him," said Nolan.

"On God," said Jake.

They both burst into laughter as the tardy bell rang.

In the locker room where Sophie is still crying, a group of 3 girls walks in laughing.

"Ugh, why are you here weirdo?" said one of the girls

"Just leave me alone Tia!" yelled Sophie.

"Sophie, Belle's not here to protect you now so last time I'm saying this, leave," said Tia

Sophie responded with a bird inciting the girls' anger.

"Girls let's show her what happens to people that don't belong here," said Tia calmly.

The girls surrounded Sophie and started attacking; pushing, shoving, kicking, kneeing into her while all she could do was tuck and protect her head. But in a few hits, Sophie was knocked out and bruised from the beatdown from the group of girls.

"What should we do with her?" asked one of the girls

"Well, isn't it obvious? Let's stuff her into one of the lockers!" said Tia, with a grin on her face.

CHAPTER 2

A Lucky Discovery

Nolan is sitting in Mr. Tus' classroom waiting for the clock to hit the 5 o'clock mark. So what felt like an eternity instantly stopped when the clock struck 5.

"So Mr. Hardy, I assume you learned your lesson?" asked Mr. Tus.

"Yes sir, I sure did," said Nolan

"Alright, you're good to go," said Mr. Tus

"Thank you," said Nolan

Nolan grabbed his bag and left the classroom prepared to leave immediately.

"Dick," said Nolan under his breath.

His pacing was interrupted and he heard screams coming from across the hall. As he listened to the screams, he recognized Sophie's voice and immediately rushed down into the female locker rooms.

"Sophie!" cried Nolan.

"Over here!" yelled Sophie.

Nolan pulled the locker door as hard as he can, eventually opening the door and releasing Sophie from her prison.

"You alright!?" asked Nolan

"If I see her again, her face is going to require plastic surgery!" said Sophie angrily.

"Believe me, she already looked bad before she

had surgery on her nose. But for now, let's get the hell out of here," said Nolan.

"You're right, I'm tired," replied Sophie, fixing her messy dark hair.

Sophie and Nolan walked outside of the school but that is where they see that the entrance gate is already locked up.

"Aww man, don't tell me Mr. Tus's ass already locked up the gate," said Nolan.

"We could just go through the woods," suggested Sophie.

Nolan looked surprised and replied "The woods? But that's where they found Sophie's dead b-

"I know! But Mr. Tus took away all my research papers so this is the perfect opportunity to make up for that," said Sophie.

"If you say so," replied Nolan.

The two teenagers turned their direction towards the woods and started walking inside, unknowingly about to make an amazing discovery. During their journey, Nolan and Sophie took a much-needed break as they were walking for half an hour, with no end in sight.

"I can't believe we're lost," said Sophie

"Even worse, the cell phone signal here is crap so I can't call nobody," said Nolan

"Ohmygod," said Sophie. "I wanted to find something that could help me find Belle's murderer."

"Sophie," said Nolan

"But maybe Mr. Tus was right, I'm in over my head," said Sophie.

"Sophie!" said Nolan.

With her hands over her head, Sophie continued "Belle was the first person to talk to me after I moved down here, I only knew her for 2 years and she was already the best friend I could ask for. She didn't show any signs of being suicidal, or what if I didn't notice any of them? What kind of friend am I?"

"SOPHIE!" yelled out Nolan.

"What!?" replied Sophie.

Nolan pointed toward her direction and said "What's that shiny thing near your foot?"

Sophie looked down and saw a golden-pinkish phone case beside her foot, with most of it being covered with leaves and dirt. Bending down, Sophie picked up the phone case and stared at it, hard, really hard.

"It's her phone," said Sophie with a smile.

"That's great but could we hurry up and get out of here?" said Nolan

"Oh yeah, we need to get out and figure out what to do next," said Sophie happily.

Sophie put the phone in her bag and continued with Nolan on their journey back home.

That night at Sophie's house, she and Nolan sit at the table pondering on what to do next with the discovery of Belle's phone.

"I still can't believe it!" yelled Sophie excitedly.

"Yeah, look like it's a good thing that Mr. Tus took your papers and you got beat up," said Nolan.

7

"I wouldn't say that now," said Sophie rolling her eyes... "Anyways is the phone charged up yet?"

"It's at 4 percent," said Nolan.

"Ugh! What's taking forever for it to charge? said Sophie annoyed.

"We literally just came back 5 minutes ago, it has been almost a hour since we found that phone," said Nolan.

Walking from the kitchen, a slim middle-aged woman comes and sets a plate of cookies on the table.

"Thanks, Ms. Struss," said Nolan.

"What's the occasion?" asked Sophie.

"Well you have been gone for a while, young woman. So I'm sure you must be famished, but on the other hand, I see you finally brought home a guy," replied Ms. Struss.

"Mom, it's not like that," said Sophie blushing.

Ms. Struss replied, "Oh no worries, I'll leave you two lovebirds alone, just as long as y'all don't have-"

"Mom!" cried Sophie.

"I'm leaving," said Ms. Struss as she's walking away.

"I don't believe she's your mom, you two are complete opposites," said Nolan.

"She's been that happy ever since she started seeing a new guy," replied Sophie.

"Oooo, you gonna have a step-dad?," said Nolan mockingly.

"Oh shut up, I haven't even met him yet," said

Sophie taking a bite of a cookie. "So what percent is the phone on?"

"It's at 9 percent now," replied Nolan.

"Great! That's good enough. Turn it on." said Sophie excitedly.

Nolan turns on the phone to reveal a blank wallpaper as it finishes loading.

"That's not right," said Sophie. "Let me see."

As Nolan passed the phone over to Sophie who had a worried look on her face, Nolan already knew the most plausible outcome.

"This can't be right," Sophie said, staring at the phone. "There's nothing on it."

"What?" said Nolan.

After a minute of exploring Belle's phone, Sophie sighed disappointedly.

"Man, when I thought I finally got a lead." said Sophie.

BUZZ

Sophie and Nolan turn their eyes to the buzzing noise which was coming from the phone.

Noticing that the number isn't recognized, Sophie picked up the phone. "Hello." she calmly said.

"It's about time you answered."

"Yeah, I've been busy." lied Sophie

"Well I got a notification that this phone just been reactivated, I was hoping we could meet up at my house."

"Okay, sure thing. I'll be available tomorrow.," said Sophie

"Perfect, I'll send you my address. I'll see you tomorrow."

"Great, I'll see you tomorrow as well," said Sophie.

Sophie hung up the phone and turned towards Nolan who was sporting a worried look on his face.

"Who was that?" asked Nolan.

"It was from someone who knew we got Belle's phone," said Sophie. They asked to meet us at their place and I said yes."

"Sophie what the hell!" exclaimed Nolan spitting out his cookie. "This wasn't part of the plan!"

"But for now this is our only lead to finding who killed Belle," replied Sophie.

"I wasn't planning on getting killed either!" said Nolan.

"But if they knew Belle, then they must be close to one another. Nolan please, help me with this mission, I need to find out who killed Belle. I'll do anything!" pleaded Sophie.

Nolan sighed. "First, I want 10 dollars."

"Deal," said Sophie, pulling a bill out of her purse.

"Hold up," said Nolan. "A date maybe?"

"No." said Sophie.

"Okay, another $10," said Nolan

"Okay." sighed Sophie. "You drive right?"

"I have a learners' permit," said Nolan.

"Great. We'll meet here tomorrow and go to this man's house and find out who killed Belle," said Sophie.

"I'm pretty sure it won't be that easy but sure," said Nolan.

Ms. Struss enters the living room dressed up in a nice dress. "Alright, I'm going out tonight so behave yourselves. But on the other hand, it would be nice to have some grandchildren."

"MOM!!" yelled Sophie.

CHAPTER 3

Revelation

It is afternoon the next day, Sophie is standing outside her house waiting for Nolan to arrive. All that is currently on Sophie's mind is finding out the identity of the mysterious caller and their relation to Belle. A white truck pulled up to the driveway, prompting Sophie to put all her focus into the mission ahead of her.

"Took you long enough," said Sophie.

"Hey, I spent 20 minutes convincing my parents we weren't going to do anything nasty," said Nolan.

"It's weird how our parents always think we gonna bone," said Sophie

"Not like I didn't want to," said Nolan under his breath.

"If you don't unlock the door right now," said Sophie.

"Alright," said Nolan. "Is that a bat?"

"Yep!" said Sophie. "Can't ever be too cautious."

Nolan sighed. "Just get in."

Sophie entered the car and the two took off on their journey to the mysterious caller's house. In what seemed like a long time, the two finally arrived at their location which was shocking to them. This is because the house was in a suburban neighborhood covered with plants and flowers.

"Are you sure this is the correct place?" asked Nolan. "Not as scary as I thought it would be."

"Can't be too sure," said Sophie. "Follow me."

The two exited out the truck and with Sophie's bat in hand, they walked up to the door knocking on it slowly preparing for the worst.

A voice came through the door "Who is it?" said in a deep voice.

"Um... we were invited over here," said Nolan.

Sophie and Nolan were terrified and were prepared to run or use the bat, depending on who this person turned out to be.

The door opened to reveal a middle-aged woman dressed in grey attire.

"You must be Sophie," said the woman.

"Yes, how do you know my name?" asked Sophie cautiously.

"I'll explain but first, come inside, both of you and leave the bat. I suppose I wasn't as scary as you thought." said the woman meekly.

Sophie dropped the bat on the ground with Nolan and walked into the woman's house which was littered with pill bottles and beer cans.

"Have a seat," said the woman, which Sophie and Nolan complied with.

"So first things first, you should know I am the ex-wife of your teacher, Mr. Tus. But you may call me, Ms. Lana."

Sophie and Nolan looked at each other with a surprised look.

"So he told you about me, I'm guessing," said Sophie.

"Honestly Sophie, it's hard not to. He legitimately pities you because of your obsession with finding Belle's supposed murderer," replied Ms. Lana laughingly.

"But answer me this, how and why do you have her number?" asked Sophie sternly.

"Oh Sophie, even though you were her best friend, there's a lot about Belle you don't know," said Ms. Lana.

"So, why did you call us then?" asked Nolan.

Ms. Lana stood still for a minute before resuming. "Listen, the main reason I divorced my husband was because he cheated on me with Belle."

"Bullshit!" cried Sophie.

"Ms. Struss, I am too old to make such a stupid lie. Also think, why else would I have her number? If you don't believe me, check her emails." said Ms. Lana.

"But all her information has been erased," said Nolan.

"Oh child, nothing on the internet can ever be truly erased. Well if you have her account information, I'm sure the two of y'all could find what y'all are looking for," replied Ms. Lana.

"Do you know who killed her?" asked Sophie.

Ms. Lana smiled at the question. "Oh Sophie, do-"

"Answer the question!? Do you know who killed her?" asked Sophie.

Ms. Lana sighed. "Honestly, I do not know. But if you're so hellbent on finding who might have killed Belle, check her emails. If you're really her best friend, you should know,"

Nolan noticed Sophie's anger was rising. "Uh, thanks Ms. Lana for the info, but we're gonna head out."

"Okay children, take care. But believe me, Ms. Struss, you will not like the truth of who Belle really is," said Ms. Lana.

Nolan hurriedly ushered Sophie out the door before she could do anything reckless. Shutting the door behind them, the two walked back into the truck.

"Dude, how someone like Mr. Tus get to hit it and not me?" said Nolan.

Sophie shot Nolan a death glare.

"I meant Ms. Lana, not Belle." said Nolan. "So what now?" he asked.

"We'll see tomorrow," said Sophie.

CHAPTER 4

What Friends Are For

Monday morning at Whitewood High School, Sophie and Nolan are in the cafeteria discussing what to do about Belle's emails and her alleged relationship with Mr. Tus.

"I'm telling you, Sophie, let's go to the police and be done with it," said Nolan.

"I don't exactly have a good reputation, plus Mr. Tus been working here for 15 years so I don't think they're gonna believe us," said Sophie.

"Oh yeah, also we might prove that he was a creep, but not responsible for Belle's murder." said Nolan.

"It makes sense," said Sophie. "If he was dating Belle, then when his ex-wife found out, he feared that it would become public and ruin his career. So he killed Belle by poisoning her, which is why she doesn't have any wounds and thus his career can be saved."

"That's actually a smart theory," said Nolan surprised. "But how are we supposed to find her emails?"

"I know her email username but not her password," said Sophie. "So if we find a hacker then we should be able to see her emails."

"But how are we gonna convince any of these nerds to help us?" asked Nolan.

Sophie smirked. "I'm gonna charm them into helping us."

Nolan laughed at the response.

Sophie rolled her eyes at his laughter. "Oh wait till the end of school today, we should have at least 5 hackers working with us. "We'll meet up in the library after school."

"Alright," said Nolan.

At 3:30, Nolan is sitting in the library with Jake waiting for Sophie and her "hacker".

"So you really joined that weirdo Sophie on that dumb quest to find Belle's murderer?" asked Jake.

"Yes because that's what friends are for, also I'm pretty sure she's gonna get herself killed without me," replied Nolan.

"Dude, you can do better," said Jake, shaking his head.

"I'm here!" yelled Sophie, entering the library.

"Where's the hacker you supposedly seduced?" asked Nolan.

"Oh he's coming there he is," said Sophie, pointing towards the door.

Entering the library comes an overweight kid, with messy hair and prickly skin.

"Hey... I'm Conor, um...it's nice to meet you," he said.

Jake laughed loudly. "Of course this is the only person you can charm. Y'all have fun now 'cause I have a hot date with Tia."

With that, Jake grabbed his backpack and left still laughing, angering the librarian.

"So Conor, since you're a freshman and all, are you familiar with Belle Frank?" asked Sophie.

"Um...I heard that she was popular and nice then suddenly she killed herself," replied Conor.

"But here's the thing, the chemistry teacher, Mr. Tus was dating her secretly and killed her to keep it secret," said Sophie.

"Still a theory though," said Nolan.

"Shut up Nolan," said Sophie. "See Conor, that where you come in, we need you to hack into her email account so we prove that Belle was murdered by Mr. Tus."

"I'll see what I can do," said Conor.

Conor took out his laptop from his backpack and opened it.

"Alright, what's her email username," asked Conor.

"It's southernbelle473@gmail.com" said Sophie.

"Um...any idea what her password might be?" said Conor.

"Huh, honestly no," said Sophie surprised.

"Um...it should take me about a week give or take," said Conor.

Sophie stood there and Nolan took notice of that.

"Well, Caleb-"

"Oh it's Conor," said Conor.

"Conor whatever, thanks for helping and I guess

we'll meet one week from now." said Nolan.

"Um... okay, I'll try my best," said Conor.

Conor began putting up his laptop and Nolan walked to him.

"How did she pay you to do this?" whispered Nolan.

"Um... she offered 5 dollars," replied Conor.

"Hmm, okay," said Nolan.

As Conor left, Nolan looked at Sophie who was still standing there in deep thought.

"You okay?" asked Nolan.

"I'm fine, I just don't know what her password might be," said Sophie.

Sophie flashed back to what Ms. Lana said about how as Belle's best friend, she should at least have a clue as to what her password would be.

"Well, hey look on the bright side, you found a hacker and we're gonna find her emails," said Nolan.

"But still..." replied Sophie.

"Don't worry 'bout it, I don't even know Jake's password and besides, we deserve a break. We already found Belle's phone, we'll just let that fat kid do the rest for now," said Nolan.

"Yeah, you're right. I'll take it easy while he's busy with her email account," said Sophie.

"That's good," said Nolan, who was packing up his backpack.

"Thank you," said Sophie.

"For what?" asked Nolan.

"For helping me on this dumb quest," said

Sophie jokingly.

"That's what friends are for," replied Nolan.

"You know, how about we get ice cream to celebrate when this is over." said Sophie.

"Sounds like a plan." replied Nolan.

CHAPTER 5

Evidence

A week passed by, since the meeting at the library. Sophie is walking to Mr. Tus' classroom as the tardy bell is about to ring.

"Sophie, it looks like you haven't been tardy at all this week," said Mr. Tus. "I'm betting you're glad about our little conversation last Friday."

Sophie ignored him and simply went straight to her seat. She cared nothing about being on time, she needed to be there to look for any suspicious activity.

BUZZ

Sophie looked down at her phone to see a text notification from Conor that read "I got in."

Later after school in the library, Sophie, Nolan, and Conor gathered around the laptop displaying Belle's emails.

"Scroll down," said Sophie to which Conor complied.

After passing many college invitations, letters from loved ones, and magazine subscriptions Sophie instantly noticed "Tus" in her inbox.

"Hold on," said Sophie. She pointed to the tab and turned to Conor "Click on that one." she said.

Conor clicked on the tab which showed the letter

sent to her which read:

Belle, I know about your disgusting relationship with Mr. Tus. I just told his wife and she is very heartbroken. Someone like you deserves what's coming. Now, what if, I told your best friend, your parents or the rest of the school? Now if you want to maintain your good, innocent reputation meet me ALONE at the abandoned cabin in the woods outside of the school tonight.

Below the text, were 2 photos showing Belle and Mr. Tus inside his classroom hugging.

Sophie looked in utter disgust, followed by Nolan.

"Hot," said Conor

"Gross," said Sophie

"Great! We got all the evidence we need to report Mr. Tus to the cops," said Nolan.

"Hold on, this email proves that Belle was actually murdered. We need to go to the abandoned cabin," said Sophie.

"Sophie, have you lost your mind?" asked Nolan. " Belle was found dead literally the next morning after this email was sent."

"Nolan, we've come so close right now, we can't stop," replied Sophie.

"I know that I agreed to help you, but it feels like it too much," said Nolan.

"Don't tell me you're backing out now," said Sophie.

"As I said before, I'm not trying to die," said Nolan.

"This email was sent 6 months ago so I doubt the murderer is still there," said Sophie

"Just like how Ms. Lana called us the same day we found Belle's phone after it had been dead for 6 months?" asked Nolan.

"Try not to overthink it," said Sophie.

"I ain't going," said Nolan sternly...

Sophie took a deep breath. "You know what, that's your decision and I ain't gonna fuss with you," Sophie who turned to Conor. "What about you, Conor?"

"Conway, I mean Caleb, damn it! Conor, tell her that this is suicide." said Nolan.

"Um... I ain't got nothing else to do so I'll go with Sophie," said Conor.

"Well good luck," said Nolan sarcastically, walking away.

"Fine," said Sophie.

"Fine," said Nolan.

"Fine!" said Sophie.

"FINE!" said Nolan.

"SHHH!" said the librarian aggressively.

At 5pm at Sophie's house, Sophie and Conor discuss how to proceed in sneaking into the abandoned cabin.

"So then I'll say that we are going to get ice cream," said Sophie.

"Um...I'm guessing that's when we are going to

sneak into the cabin," said Conor.

"Yep!" said Sophie.

"But what are we looking for, exactly?" asked Conor.

Sophie replied "Alright so since Belle didn't have any wounds on her corpse, I can guess that Mr. Tus being a chemistry teacher poisoned her so that means…"

"Chemicals?" asked Conor

"Exactly," said Sophie smirking.

Ms. Struss walks over from the kitchen and places cookies on the table.

"Cookies, again?" sighed Sophie.

"I am going out again tonight, I need to make sure y'all won't go starving," said Ms. Struss.

"These are delicious!" said Conor.

"At least someone appreciates my cookies," said Ms. Struss. "Well, have fun you too." With that Ms. Struss leaves the house.

Sophie turns towards Conor. "Ready."

"Let me finish these cookies first," Conor replied.

Sophie sighs.

CHAPTER 6

Search

At 6 pm, Sophie and Conor are walking inside the woods nearby the school. In the dark terrain, Sophie is shining her flashlight for any sign of the cabin. Following her from behind is Conor who on the other hand is complaining of the freezing conditions.

"Ughh, I'm so cold." moaned Conor.

"Don't worry we're close," said Sophie. "I think."

"My stomach hurts." moaned Conor.

"Oh, shut up!" said Sophie. "You shouldn't have eaten all those cookies anyway."

"She shouldn't have made so many then." moaned Conor.

"Honestly, I don't know why she makes so many anyway. It started after she learned that Belle died."

"Huh. Were y'all close to Belle?" asked Conor.

"Of course, she was my best friend, and she was like a second daughter to my mom. She always loved to eat her cookies when she came over, so I guess it's her way of coping," replied Sophie.

"Oh, so that's why you're doing this," said Conor

"I think I see the cabin," said Sophie.

She points her flashlight revealing the cabin in plain sight. Cautiously, Sophie and Conor entered the cabin and shut the door, looking for any signs of chemicals. Looking through empty cabinets, drawers, and pantries, the two teenagers couldn't find anything useful for their search.

Meanwhile, at Nolan's house in his bedroom, Nolan is feeling conflicted about his actions earlier at school towards Sophie. He then calls Jake to clear his conscience.

"Yo what's up man?" asked Jake.

"Dude, I feel bad," said Nolan.

"This about Sophie again?" asked Jake.

"Yep," said Nolan.

"Dude, Imma make this quick because me and Tia are about to get busy. I know I said you can do better, but if she makes you feel good then I guess you don't need to do better," said Jake.

"That's got to be the most non-dickish thing you ever said," said Nolan jokingly.

"Nah, I stole that from a TV show. Gotta go, she's getting impatient," said Jake.

After hanging up with Jake, Nolan felt inclined to go meet up with Sophie and Conor. So he hurriedly put on a jacket, shoes and soon left home to meet up with his friends.

"Sophie, take a look at this," said Conor.

Sophie went over to Conor to see what he had found, which was a folded piece of paper with Belle's username written on the front.

BANG!

The loud sudden noise startled Sophie and Conor, but the scarier part for them was seeing a new hole in the walls that were not there before.

"OH SH-" cried Conor before his mouth got covered by Sophie's hand.

Sophie knew immediately that they were trapped as there was one entrance and exit. The cabin only contains a single room meaning there is limited space to hide. Sophie moved herself and Conor who is currently panicking to a corner to limit the possibility of being shot. Grabbing her phone knowing that the police won't find them before it's too late, she made an impulsive decision.

Nolan answered "Hi Sophie, I'm coming towards y-"

"I'm about to die and I need you to tell my mom I love her." hurried Sophie.

"What's happening?" said Nolan.

"There's someone trying to shoot us." said Sophie.

"Hold on, Sophie, I need you to open the door." said Nolan.

"What?" asked Sophie.

"Don't worry I got a plan," said Nolan.

Against her better judgement, Sophie carefully walked towards the door and pushed on it. It slammed open when a masked figure walked in holding a gun.

WHACK!

The masked figure fell to the floor, revealing a man carrying a bat, no one other than Nolan.

"Nolan!" exclaimed Sophie relived.

"You left this in my truck," said Nolan.

"So I was right to bring a bat," said Sophie.

"Can't ever be too cautious," said Nolan.

"Stealing my lines now?" asked Sophie.

"You know you still owe me $10 right?" said Nolan.

"I'll use it to pay for the ice cream," said Sophie.

"Um...guys I don't mean to interrupt but can we please get out of here?" asked Conor.

"But first," said Sophie walking toward the masked gunman.

Sophie kicked the gun away, then pulled the mask off to reveal the gunman was no other than Ms. Lana.

"I had a feeling that it was you," said Sophie.

"Um... who is this?" asked Conor.

"This is Mr. Tus' ex-wife who he left for Belle. It was obvious from the start," said Sophie smugly.

"But how did she know y'all was here?" asked Nolan.

Sophie pulled out her phone and scrolled. "Oh yeah, she used the SnappyChat app to find my phone location."

"But that doesn't make any sense though," said Nolan. "It's usually never the most obvious suspect. She gave us hints about her emails and divorce."

"You really are overthinking stuff," said Sophie. "Anyways, I guess case closed, we finally have all the evidence. I guess you can finally call the cops-

"Not...yet." said Ms. Lana who is now bleeding from her head. "Despite everything, I wasn't the one who killed Belle."

"Then who the hell is it?" asked Sophie smugly.

Ms. Lana chuckled to herself.

"Oh Sophie, when did your parents divorce?" asked Ms. Lana.

"When I was three, 13 years ago. Why the hell does that matter?" asked Sophie.

"Well, I'm actually Mr. Tus's second wife," said Lana.

"What are you trying to say?" asked Sophie.

Ms. Lana smirked "Mr. Tus is your father, Sophie."

"I don't believe a damn thing you just said." said Sophie blunty. "Even if that was true, he still isn't nothing more than a teacher to me."

"But your mother loved him since she was his first wife. She was the one who found out about the affair, so she showed me pictures confirming it."

"Wait," said Sophie.

"It makes sense now doesn't it, Sophie? After inviting Belle here, she showed up dead the next morning, your mother killed Belle." said Ms. Lana.

"What proof do you have?" said scoffed Sophie.

"Call her then, if you notice, she has been going out recently," said Ms. Lana.

Sophie looked at Nolan who nodded his head and Conor who shrugged. With a semi-unanimous decision, Sophie dials her mom's number on her phone, calling to find the truth.

"Yes, sweetie?" said Ms. Struss

"Where are you at right now?" asked Sophie.

"I'm still in town, do you need anything?" replied Ms. Struss.

"Mom I need to know, are you seeing Mr. Tus?" asked Sophie.

A moment of silence erupted.

"Sophie, why do you ask?" asked Ms. Struss.

"Because I need to know. Are you seeing Mr. Tus?" said Sophie.

"Yes, I am. I see you when I get home." and hang up the phone.

"It can't be!" cried Sophie, who was now shaking.

"I told you didn't I?" said Ms. Lana mockingly, which was met with a punch from Sophie who started breaking down.

"That's it, I'm calling the cops," said Nolan.

A perfect opportunity thought Ms. Lana, so in a quick burst of energy, she ran towards the gun. But the second she ran, so did Nolan; therefore it was a race for the gun.

Ms. Lana grabs ahold of the gun, not before being punched by Nolan forcing her release on the deadly weapon. While grabbing the gun, he tried pointing towards Ms. Lana who seemed to have disappeared from his view.

CLANK

Using the bat, Ms. Lana hit Nolan from behind.

"AAHHHH!!!" Nolan screamed, in pain, so he released the gun which was thrown into the ground.

Ms. Lana grabbed the gun and pointed towards Sophie, who was still in a breakdown.

Nolan hurried got back up and ran to Ms. Lana in an attempt to wrestle the gun from her.

BANG

CHAPTER 7

Dark Blue

Nolan had been shot and fell to the ground.

"Nolan!" screamed Sophie.

"My bad, Nolan was it?" asked Ms. Lana. "That was meant for her."

"Why did you invite us?" said Sophie quietly.

"Pardon?" said Ms. Lana.

"You heard me, bitch!" yelled Sophie. "We wouldn't have gotten her emails if you hadn't told us!"

"But if you must know, I wanted you to find them. My ex-husband deserves to rot in jail, but the reason I'm targeting you is much more complex. You see, your mother knows that you are capable of solving this case on your own, which will blow our cover. You see, she planned on poisoning you and your friends with cookies. So instead of ending up like Belle, I decided to give all of you a much more dignified end."

Pointing her gun towards Sophie. "But I give you this, you completed your goal of finding who murdered Belle."

WHAM

Ms. Lana was knocked into the wall by Conor who then ran towards Sophie and Nolan.

"Are you alright?" asked Conor.

"My chest is burning." moaned Nolan.

"I'll carry you," said Conor. "Do you have the evidence, Sophie?"

"Yeah, I got the note, we can go," said Sophie. "But one last thing," she said, walking towards Ms. Lana who was writhing in pain with a closed fist.

POW!

Elsewhere in a house, Jake and Tia were engaged in pillow-talk when,

BUZZ

"Hold on, it's Nolan," Jake said to Tia while picking up his phone.

"What's up man?"

"Hey!" said Sophie.

"Sophie? asked Jake surprised. " Are you and Nolan slee-"

"Nolan just been shot, you need to come now!" exclaimed Sophie.

Jake jumped out of bed immediately, starling Tia.

"Where are y'all at?" asked Jake.

"We're on South Avenue Rd outside the forest near the abandoned cabin," said Sophie.

"I'm on my way," said Jake.

"Thanks," said Sophie who then hung up.

Sophie looks down at Nolan who was lying on the ground asleep.

"Wouldn't an ambulance be faster though?" asked Conor.

"Yeah but we can't afford it, plus we're gonna have to explain why we were sneaking on private property." said Sophie.

"Oh yeah, that would bring up some questions," said Conor. "By the way, what that woman said, do you believe your mom really killed Belle?"

"Honestly I can't believe it but, I'm gonna have to talk to her myself," said Sophie.

"I see," said Conor.

A grey car blasting loud music pulled up and stopped, rolling down the windows, it was Jake.

"Jake to the rescue!" said Jake.

"Why are you shirtless?" asked Conor.

"Because unlike you, I was getting laid," said Jake smugly.

"Okay, Jake, what is taking the hell so long?" said a female voice.

"Tia for the last time, bros before hoes," said Jake.

"Why the hell are you here? asked Sophie. "You don't even like us."

"I know I was a teeny tiny bit of a bitch to you, but I do have a heart," said Tia.

"Tiny is a real understatement," said Sophie.

"Well, I admitted I was a teeny tiny bit wrong. Ugh, stop being so negative." Tia replied.

"SOPHIE!!"

"Oh no, she's awake!" yelled Conor.

"Who?" said Jake.

"It's a long story," said Sophie.

"Well hurry and get Nolan's ass in," said Jake.

Sophie and Conor helped carry Nolan into the car then got inside themselves. But before the car door was shut, Ms. Lana ran out of the forest and pointed her gun to the car.

BANG

"Oh shit!" yelled Jake who then slammed on the gas.

Ms. Lana tried running after the car in a futile attempt to catch up to them but was easily left behind.

"Nolan. Nolan. Nolan." said Sophie.

Nolan opened his eyes to see he was in Jake's car along with Tia, Sophie, and Conor.

"What happened?" said Nolan groggily.

"We're taking your ass to a hospital," said Jake.

"By the way, be sure to tell everyone that we saved your life," said Tia.

"Huh?" said Nolan who then unzipped his jacket to reveal a big red stain over his white t-shirt.

"Aw man, my parents ain't gonna let go out no more." said Nolan disappointedly.

"But it's over now, I suppose," said Sophie. "I guess I'll have to turn in my mom."

"Sophie," said Nolan before grunting in pain.

"It's fine," said Sophie. "I just need to talk to her alone."

"Okay," said Nolan.

CHAPTER 8
Un-Revelation

The next day, at the hospital Sophie and Nolan's parents are sitting in the waiting room for Nolan's prognosis.

"I am once again sorry for what happened to Nolan," said Sophie.

"It wasn't your fault, we've just glad you both are still alive," said Ms. Hardy

"But then again, I can't believe that Mr. Tus' ex-wife would break into your house, and hold you, hostage," said Mr. Hardy.

"I can't believe it either," replied Sophie, because she knew that was not what happened.

Sophie remembered after arriving at the hospital, she and Jake carried Nolan to E.R. where they immediately started surgery on him. When asked how this occurred, Sophie claims that Ms. Lana broke into their house and held them hostage. Nolan was shot, protecting her giving her and Conor time to escape. They happened to see Jake and Tia driving by their house, where they stopped and helped take Nolan to the hospital.

Sophie looks at the clock, waiting for the doctor to come out and announce the results. But then there was a knock on the door, two men entered the room but Sophie knew why they were here.

"Ms. Sophie Struss, we are detectives from the Whitewood Police Department. We need you for questioning regarding last night's incident."

"But she didn't do anything wrong," said Ms. Hardy.

"No, I understand, I'll go," said Sophie.

Then Sophie grabbed her bag and went with the police detectives, who then escorted her to the police station. Placed in a room for questioning, Sophie wondered if she should come clean.

"Alright, Sophie Struss." said a man entering the room.

"My name is David Bowle, and I want to hear your official side of the story."

Sophie said, "Well, I was at my house with Nolan and Conor when Ms. Tucker broke inside and then-"

"I'm going to have to stop you right there," said Officer Bowle. "Your mother said that she saw Ms. Lana during the time of the supposed break-in. Along with that, our detectives went to your house and found no signs of forced entry nor escape."

Sophie could only look at Officer Bowle, trying to think of an explanation for the "break-in".

Officer Bowle continued, "Sophie, I can tell you're hiding something, if you had done anything illegal, go ahead and confess in hopes of a possible misdemeanor charge. But if you haven't done anything wrong, either you have been threatened not to tell us or you are protecting someone."

Sophie bowed her head in defeat, knowing

that she would have to tell them the whole story, including her mother.

"Sophie!" said Ms. Struss who opened and came through the door.

"Mom?" said Sophie.

Officer Bowle turns towards Ms. Struss "Excuse me, ma'am, we are busy ri-"

"Excuse me sir, my daughter had been stressed out all day!" exclaimed Ms. Struss. "Her friend has been shot, and on top, she was interrogated for hours. Could she at least talk with her mother?"

Officer Bowle sighed, "Ten minutes." leaving the room with just Sophie and Ms. Struss.

Sophie turned towards her mother, "Mom, did you-"

"No, please don't listen to anything that nut job Lana told you," said Ms. Struss. "I'm just glad you're safe," she said hugging Sophie.

Sophie pushed her away, "Mom, tell me the truth." she said.

Ms. Struss gave a depressed look, "I'll tell you everything. Have a seat because this will be a lot to take in."

"It was about a year ago, you and Belle we're working on a project for chemistry, which I think was to create a 30-slide presentation for finals."

1 Year Ago

"I can't believe we actually finished that," said *Sophie.*

"Of course, with just the two of us, anything's possible," replied Belle.

"So all we have to do is just turn in, and summer' here we come," said Sophie.

"Sounds like a plan," closing the laptop, said Belle. "I'll go ahead and turn it into him."

"Okay, I'll be waiting at home later on," said Sophie.

Walking towards Mr. Tus' classroom, Belle slips and drops her laptop onto the floor.

"Ohmygod, please be alright." Belle whispered to herself, collecting herself and continuing her pace towards Mr. Tus' classroom."

"Hey, Mr. Tus, here's mine and Sophie's project," said Belle, entering the classroom.

"Great, let me take a look at it," said Mr. Tus.

"Here," said Belle, pushing her laptop towards Mr. Tus.

Mr. Tus looked at the laptop for a few seconds.

"There's nothing but a cracked screen," said Mr. Tus.

"What?" asked Belle.

Belle pulls the laptop towards her, showing a black cracked screen.

"Oh my God," said Belle. "Mr. Tus, could you please give us an extra day to make up for this?" she asked.

"I'm sorry but all finals are due today, no exceptions." Mr. Tus replied.

Belle immediately said, "But we just finished a while ago, and I slipped and broke my laptop, and-

"No exceptions, no matter the reason," said Mr. Tus.

"But we'll fail!" cried Belle.

"Not my problem, sorry," said Mr. Tus.

"I'll do anything! Please, Mr. Tus, I'll do anything you ask me for if you could give us one more day!" cried Belle.

"Anything?" asked Mr. Tus.

"Yes!" cried Belle.

At that moment, Belle had made the worst decision of her life. But at first, it seemed simple, a kiss for an automatic A on y'all finals. But over the next few days, Tus has been craving that passion and suddenly started needing to talk to Belle after class, every other day. Soon enough, I noticed that each time she came to visit, she'd visibly lost a bit of weight. Worried, I would always bake a fresh batch of cookies for her to eat, not by choice. I started getting suspicious and so, one day I went up to the office at y'all school and asked where I could find Belle. So after they gave me the direction for Tus's classroom, I went to knock on the door. Before I did knock, through the window I saw both Belle and Thus being affectionate towards each other. I took pictures on my phone and went straight back to the office, but unfortunately, my phone died before I could say anything incriminating. I just left, and went straight home where after recharging my phone I sent an email to Tus's wife, Lana using the photos as confirmation. Little did I know, that was a grave mistake as well. So I waited till she came

Albert Cooper III

over and visited, while you were in your room, I sat her down as asked for her story. Of course, she tried making up a lie but as soon as I showed her the pictures, she broke down, telling me the whole truth. I was horrified, what was supposed to be a one-time deal became a common occurrence. Belle revealed that she tried starving herself to try to turn off Tus, but it never worked. After comforting her for a few minutes, I convinced her to break it off with Tus the next day, and we'll go to the police. After that conversation, Belle was excited to start a new chapter in her life. But, the next day while getting ready to go to the police station, Belle arrives in an emotional state. I asked her what's wrong, but what she told me changed the whole situation.

"He violated me."

I started seeing in shades of red, I told Belle to spend time with you. But she said she didn't want to worry you and then asked what was planning on doing. While going to the kitchen, I was getting ingredients from the cabinet, that was when she asked once again what I was planning on doing. I calmly told her that I was going to kill Tus. Belle tried to convince me to just go to the police station, but I wanted him to suffer. So using all the regular ingredients with a "pinch" of rat poison, I baked a fresh batch of cookies that would cause agonizing pain and eventually killed whoever ate it. I forced Belle to spend time with you so I drove to Tus's residence. Before getting out, I looked at my phone and saw that Ms. Tus replied to my email; looking at it read,

Ms. Struss, I can't believe my husband would do such a thing. I do need to talk to you. Please meet me at the public library at 5 pm.

After reading that I redirected my car to Whitewood Public Library for which I met Ms. Tus or Ms. Lana. I told her the whole story, exactly how Belle said to me. She said she was shocked but not surprised, so I asked her to elaborate. Lana then told me about how Tus would cheat on her with young women, during the majority of their marriage. So then I foolishly told her about my plan to kill Tus by the poisonous cookies I made. Lana agreed to help me not for vengeance, but so she can collect his funds and acquire enough wealth to leave Whitewood. So we began a friendship, discussing our plan for killing Tus.

So this was the plan, Lana would send a threatening email towards Belle. She would go to the abandoned cabin where I will meet Belle. This was supposed to be a distraction, as Lana will feed her husband the poisoned cookies. So, while Tus is in agonizing pain, Lana was supposed to go to the store for an alibi. That way, we can kill Tus, get the money, and Belle can move on with her life. But it didn't go as planned, so I want you to listen closely.

After Lana sent the email, I went up to my designated spot in the abandoned cabin. I was waiting for Belle the moment that email was sent, but I didn't see her for hours. I called Belle on my phone to which she never answered so I called

Lana to which she answered,

"Oh Trista, is Belle up there with you?" asked Lana.

"No, not yet, have you fed Tus the cookies?" I asked.

"He didn't eat them at that moment, but he took some to school for his meeting," replied Lana.

"Okay, that's good. I'll call my daughter and see if she's at my house." I said,

As I hung up the phone and called you, I was given the worst possible news at that moment. I hung up the phone and called Lana back.

Lana answered, "So is Belle at-

"She's at school," I said,

"What!?" yelled Lana.

"Sophie said she had to finish work for Tus," I said,

"Shit!" cried Lana. "Trista I'm on my way, meet me there."

"I'm on my way," I said,

So I hurried into my car and drove off to the school. When I arrived, I noticed Lana was already there so I got out and hurried to catch up with her. After running to the school and through the hallways, I finally arrived at Tus's classroom. When I entered, I saw something that I can never forget. Belle lying unconscious on the floor, with Mr. Tus standing over her. Beside me was Lana, who was sorrowfully looking at the scene.

"Is she dead?" I asked quietly.

"I don't know. How much poison did you put into

these cookies?" said Mr. Tus.

"No," I cried sadly.

As I realized what happened, I broke down in regret, sorrow, and agony. Lana was shocked but showed no emotion, so she was still standing.

"Did she tell you?" asked Lana.

"No.," said Mr. Tus. "You see, while you were in the shower I happened to stumble upon your phone. There, I read the conversations you two were having, plotting to kill me."

"Bastard!" cried Lana. "You cheated on me many times, but now you go after a 15-year-old girl! I always just accepted it before, causing me to get on medication because of how unloved I felt! So yes, I tried to kill you so I can get enough money to leave this damn city!"

Mr. Tus laughed to himself, prompting Lana to walk over and slap him. Mr. Tus held up his phone, pressing a button that played Lana's confession. He recorded us, so we had no power over him and he said he'll make a deal with us. The deal was me and Lana will carry Belle's corpse into the woods and write a suicide note that we will plant in the cabin. That is where Lana threw Belle's phone as far away as possible in the woods. Then, Lana was forced to get a divorce, in so preventing any chance of his wealth getting passed onto her. Next, I am required to go with him on dates whenever he calls me. I thought that was the worst night of my life but yet, the next day when a hiker found her body. Aside from her elderly mother who had dementia, the next person who learned of her death was you. Being indirectly responsible for her death was a feeling I can never shake off. But seeing your reaction to the news, it was the worst feeling a mother can ever feel. You stopped taking care of yourself; stopped showering, stopped eating, and isolating yourself. I felt like I betrayed you and ultimately failed as a mother, so in my opinion, that was the worst day of my life."

But four months ago, you were severely depressed and like a zombie. I was afraid I would lose my other daughter too, so I said something foolish. Then when I told you, that Belle didn't commit suicide. When you asked how I'd known, I simply said if you believe she didn't, then she didn't. That was when I encouraged you to solve it for her and mainly for you to get closure. Suddenly, the light came back into your eyes and you became motivated, obsessed with finding Belle's murderer. You started taking care of yourself again so I was moderately happy. But on the other hand, Lana didn't get better after her divorce with Tus. Lana and I still talked somewhat, but each time she would drift off-topic or talk about getting revenge on Tus. Without Tus's income, Lana couldn't afford her medications so her mental state has gotten worse. Two weeks ago, when you brought home Belle's phone which I wiped clean, I was confused about what to do. Having no other person to discuss it with, I called Lana about the discovery. She assured me that she would take care of it, asking for Belle's number, as

"Mom, no," said Sophie.

The door opens with Officer Bowle and two other policemen entering the room.

"Ms. Trista Struss, stand up and put your hands over your head." said one of the policemen.

"No," said Sophie.

Ms. Struss stood up and compiled, putting her hands over her head where she was handcuffed.

"No.," said Sophie with tears now running down her face.

"I'm so proud of you," said Ms. Struss.

"No!" exclaimed Sophie who stood up.

"I love you Sophie," said Ms. Struss who was being led out of the room.

Sophie sits down in her chair and bitterly weeps.

CHAPTER 9

Forgetfully

At Whitewood High School, rumors were spreading centered around Nolan. In the algebra teacher, Ms. Notte's classroom, there is a discussion that is transpiring.

"So you're telling me that you got to hang out with sophomores?!" said a nerdy kid.

"Yes, Jimmy I finally got to hang out with the popular kids," said Conor happily.

"Including that hot junior Tia?" asked Jimmy.

"Um...let me pull it up," said Conor while scrolling on his phone. He then showed Jimmy a picture of a selfie with him, Jake and Tia posing.

"Dude, how did you convince her to take those pictures?" asked Jimmy.

"Um...she said if I let her and Jake have all the credit for saving Nolan, then she'll take a picture of us together. Yeah, Sophie wasn't happy about that," said Conor.

"You should've asked for a booty pic!" exclaimed Jimmy.

"Why didn't I think of that?" said Conor slapping himself on the head.

"Missed opportunity," said Jimmy shaking his head. "So any way that dude who got shot,-

"Nolan?" said Conor.

"Yeah, so do you know who shot him?" asked Jimmy.

Conor pulled Jimmy to his ear and whispered "It was Mr. Tus' ex-wife."

"No way," said Jimmy. "You gotta tell me the whole story."

Conor took a breath and said rapidly in one breath "So basically after that sophomore Belle killed herself, Sophie, her best friend recruited me and her I guess, boyfriend Nolan, where we found that she and Mr. Tus was boning and his ex-wife finds us and shoots Nolan while he and Sophie were flirting so then told us that Sophie's mom poisoned Belle and Mr. Tus was her dad then I ran and knocked her to the wall where then I carried Nolan out of the woods while Sophie called Jake and Tia to pick us up. So then they pick us up and that where Mr. Tus's ex-wife shoots and us but we escaped before then and went to the nearby hospital where Nolan got admitted for surgery. Sophie told them a made-up story and Tia then came up to me and that is where we made our deal."

Jimmy responded with a WTF look.

"Soo... " said Jimmy. "Where is Mr. Tus's ex-wife right now?" he asked.

"I'm guessing Sophie reported her to the cops, I don't know if she got arrested or something," said Conor.

"Well, I hardly know her, but that must suck about her mom being a murderer or her dad being

Mr. Tus of all people," said Jimmy.

"Yeah, I just hope she's doing alright," said Conor.

Outside of a store in the parking lot, a car from the Whitewood Police Department arrives on the scene. Exiting the vehicle was Officer Bowle, who had a search warrant for Lana.

"Vehicle is that matches the victim's description has been spotted," said Officer Bowle.

Drawing his gun, Officer Bowle sneaked up behind the vehicle. Coming closer to the car, he noticed while the car was still running, the exhaust pipe was clogged up with a piece of cloth. He walked up to the window and saw an unconscious middle-aged woman.

"10-52, we need an ambulance!" yelled Officer Bowle who opened the car door and dragged Ms. Lana out.

Checking her heartbeat, Officer Bowle heard nothing but silence. He immediately started chest compressions on Ms. Lana who was apparently dead from carbon monoxide poisoning. As the ambulance arrived, one of the paramedics exited out and rushed to put an AED on Ms. Lana's torso.

"Clear!" shouted the paramedic.

Ms. Lana was shocked by the AED and was giving chest compressions again. After a minute of chest compressions, Ms. Lana's heart started beating again.

Opening her eyes, Ms. Lana groggily asked "Am

I dead?"

"You nearly were, until we revived you." said one of the paramedics.

"Oh no, he's gonna come after me! You have to protect me!" yelled Ms. Lana.

"Ma'am calm down." said one of the paramedics.

Officer Bowle stepped in front of her and showed his badge. "Ma'am, I'm with Whitewood Police and no one is going to harm you here. Now, I know you just have woken up but I need you to answer me these 3 questions."

"Yes, I will, I swear on my life!" exclaimed Ms. Lana.

"First," said Officer Bowle. "Did you shoot Nolan?"

"Yes, or else he would have been poisoned by Trista."

"Second," said Office Bowle. "When was the last time you took your medications?"

"It was 5 months ago, I couldn't afford them after me and Tus divorced."

"Lastly, did you see Tus standing over Belle's corpse? Along with that, did you have the email confirming their relationship?" asked Officer Bowle.

"Yes, me and Trista. The email has been deleted from my phone. I printed off the pictures, they should be located in the dashboard." said Ms. Lana.

Officer Bowle walked over to the car and opened the dashboard. Opening it, he pulled out 2 pictures of risqué photos of Mr. Tus and Belle engaged in intimacy. While attempting to hold in his disgust,

Officer Bowle called the dispatcher for an update.

"We revived Lana, we confirmed all the claims made from Trista. Also, we have a 10-96, Lana claims she hasn't taken her medications in 5 months. As for now, send units to Whitewood High School, we have a 10-91."

At Whitewood High School, in Mr. Tus's classroom, the students are presenting their projects.

"Okay Ms. Suzuki, you're next," said Mr. Tus.

Tia stood up and walked up to the front of the class. "Thank you, Mr. Tus, I dedicate this project to my dear friend Nolan, who is recovering from being shot," she said in an obviously forced caring tone.

"Yes, we heard you and Jake saved Nolan's life for the 50th time today." sighed Mr. Tus tirelessly.

"Thank you for clarifying that true statement again Mr. Tus," said Tia.

Mr. Tus sighed. "Ms. Suzuki you have 3 minutes le-"

"Okay I'm going!" exclaimed Tia. "As I was saying-

The door suddenly opens to reveal two police officers walking in, with Officer Bowle in front.

Turning toward Mr. Tus, Officer Bowle gave him a furious look and took a deep breath.

"Tus, stand up and put your hands behind your head," said Officer Bowle.

"What is this about?" asked Mr. Tus confusingly.

"I will not ask again," said Officer Bowle sternly.

Mr. Tus complied with the arresting officer who was putting handcuffs on him.

Officer Bowle said, "Tus, you are under arrest for the statutory rape and murder of Belle Frank."

"Oh shit! Sophie was right!?" yelled Tia before covering her hand over her mouth.

The reason for that was because Tia noticed another student recording the whole situation. By knowing that if she admitted Sophie solved the mystery, her popularity would fall. The damage was already done and the video the student recorded spread throughout the school.

BUZZ

"What's that?" asked Conor.

Jimmy checked his phone and looked at the notification.

"Dude, check this out," said Jimmy.

Conor looked over at Jimmy's phone to show police arresting Mr. Tus and Tia confirming it was Sophie who solved it. The two then heard a noise coming from the hallway, they turned around to see the classroom was empty. They went out the door to see students lined up on both sides of the hallway. What they saw coming from the corner was Mr. Tus being led out by police. Hurtled with profanities, trash, and offensive gestures, Mr. Tus could do nothing but stare at the ground.

"Damn brat." Mr. Tus muttered to himself.

Now the disgraced Mr. Tus is led outside to the police car, where he was taken into custody.

CHAPTER 10

Law and Power

Sophie walked out of the police department after she gave her testimony. Walking back to the hospital she checked her phone, which she hasn't used since being interrogated. Turning on her phone Sophie was surprised to see that she has received several text notifications from people she doesn't know.

"Probably just hate mail," Sophie said to herself.

Scrolling on her phone, Sophie was shocked to see the texts were positive. She read a few to herself such as,

" I was wrong about ya, you were right."

"I'm sorry for making fun of you."

"Tus's creepy-ass got arrested and they cancelled school! Thx!

Sophie then checked her social media to find that her following had grown from a mere five to over three hundred. Realizing the investigation was now public, Sophie did not know whether to be happy or nervous. Sophie felt happy to be finally validated on her 4-month quest. But then again, if they found out about her mother's involvement in Belle's murder, they might turn on her. With her newfound popularity, Sophie decided to do a risky move, and went on her social media page, and started recording herself live.

At Whitewood High School while waiting for the bus, Conor gets a notification on his phone.

"Hmm... what's this?" said Conor to himself.

Conor taps on the notification to show Sophie live on her social media page.

"Hey this is Sophie, I need your help. Some of y'all may know now that Mr. Tus is responsible for Belle's murder. But it wasn't supposed to turn out like that. You see, Belle was assaulted by him and so she told my mom who was also assaulted by him. My mom wanted to protect her and tried poisoning him but he used that against her and killed Belle and forced her to put her in the forest. My mom has turned herself in and I need your help setting her free. Please meet me at the police station and help me set her free.

As the live recording went off, Conor looked up from his phone to see that everyone else was watching the same thing. Sophie went back to the police station where they were in for a surprise.

At the Whitewood Police Department, Mr. Tus was placed in the interrogation room for questioning. Officer Bowle enters the room, carrying the photos printed off by Ms. Lana. Slamming the photos on the table, Officer Bowle got in Mr. Tus's face.

"Care to explain this?" asked Officer Bowle.

"I want a lawyer," said Mr. Tus.

"It takes a special kind of man to violate a little girl, a little girl that just happens to be my cousin!"

shouted Officer Bowle.

Mr. Tus laughed to himself silently. "And yet she was the one who ate those cookies, I merely just gave her an option," he said.

"What option?" asked Officer Bowle seriously.

"To either eat those cookies or I'll blackmail Sophie," said Mr. Tus.

Office Bowle was visibly shaking with fury.

"After I showed her proof of my resolve, she immediately took the cookies without hesitation so no, I didn't kill Belle. As you incompetent cops ruled, she simply committed suicide," said Mr. Tus.

"Listen," said Officer Bowle sternly. "My aunt, her mother has dementia. Until she died she would always ask where her only daughter was. It sickens me to lie to my aunt but seeing her die pleading for her daughter made me throw up. I swear, I will make sure you'll be sentenced to a prison where you can find all the attention you crave."

Leaving the interrogation room, Officer Bowle went to the office to file a report on the interrogation. But before he could start doing paperwork, he was greeted by his coworker, Alex.

"Micheal, you might want to see this," said Alex.

"What is it about?" asked Bowle.

"Follow me," said Alex.

Alex led Officer Bowle to the front of the police station where there was a loud chant going on. Looking through the window, the two officers saw a crowd, expecting a political protest but saw something else. It was a crowd of high school students with Sophie at the front chanting "Let her go!"

"Are they talking about La'She, Westa, or Tyla?" asked Alex.

"No, they must be talking about Trista Struss," said Office Bowle.

"But didn't she turn herself in through? So by then, technically we didn't lock her up" said Alex.

"Try not to overthink it," said Officer Bowle. "I'll talk to them," he said.

Opening the door, Officer Bowle stepped outside the station in front of the crowd of teenagers.

"Attention, attention," said Officer Bowle. "I know that you want Ms. Struss to be released, but she did break the law and will have to face the consequences for her actions."

Office Bowle was immediately met with boos and jeers after giving his statement.

"Hey, hey, hey," said Officer Bowle, trying to calm the raging crowd. "I can see that you are passionate about Ms. Struss bu-"

"She was raped by Tus!" yelled a student. "If my daughter's teacher raped my child then I would try to kill him too!

"And she didn't even kill Belle, it was Tus!" yelled another student.

"Sophie kept searching for Belle's murderer while the rest of us accepted it and made fun of her! We want to pay her back by supporting her and freeing her mom!" shouted another student.

"Enough!!" yelled Officer Bowle.

The crowd immediately went silent.

After a minute, Officer Bowle collected himself. "We will release Ms. Struss on no bail," he said.

The crowd burst into cheering after the faithful announcement.

"But," interjected Officer Bowle. "Ms. Struss is still required to go on trial for the charge of involuntary manslaughter."

Walking back in, Officer Bowle was confronted by Alex.

"What were you doing!? asked Alex. "Only a judge has the power to-"

"I'm turning in my badge after the case is closed," said Officer Bowle.

Shocked by the sudden statement, Alex could only look at Bowle who was walking towards the cells.

"Ms. Trista Struss," said Officer Bowle.

"Yes?" replied Ms. Struss

"You're free to go until you're called back for your trial," said Officer Bowle who was opening the cell.

"Hold on," said Ms. Struss puzzlingly. "How much is the bail?" she asked.

"There is no bail," replied Officer Bowle. "Your daughter is a wonderful young woman who clearly loves her mother. So much that she convinced this old sack to let you go without charge. You may go and see your daughter, she's outside waiting for you."

Holding back tears, Ms. Struss ran towards the

entrance of the police station where she saw her daughter.

"Sophie!" cried Ms. Struss.

"Mom!" cried Sophie.

The two reconciled with a big hug which was met with applause and cheering from the crowd around them.

BUZZ

Sophie noticed her phone was ringing and saw it was coming from the hospital.

"Sorry, excuse me," said Sophie excusing herself from the crowd.

"Ms. Sophie Struss?" asked the hospital receptionist.

"Yes ma'am, how's Nolan?" asked Sophie.

"I am pleased to tell you that the surgery was a success and Nolan is currently recovering right now." said the receptionist.

"Thank you," said Sophie, smiling as the line disconnected.

This was truly the happiest day of Sophie's life.

CHAPTER 11

Overthinking

Two months after the arrest of Tus, Lana, and Trista, it was time for them to face the consequences for their actions.

Starting first with Mr. Tus's trial, it was short and simple. With testimonies from Ms. Struss and photos provided by Lana, the jury took little time in reaching a verdict.

"Your honor, we the jury finds Tus guilty of both statutory rape and second-degree murder of Belle Frank." said the jury foreman.

Mr. Tus was sentenced to 15 years for statutory rape and 69 years for second-degree murder. At the request of the now-retired Officer Bowle, Tus was sent to the worst federal prison in the state to serve his sentence. Three weeks in, after numerous "shower incidents" he was found dead in his cell with his blanket wrapped around his neck.

Next was Ms. Lana, who was now mentally stable after staying in the hospital since her suicide attempt. At the trial, Lana was faced with the charge of attempted homicide. With her medical documents proving that she has a mental illness and her income confirmation she couldn't afford her medications, it was a mixed case for the jury. Having already apologized to Sophie, Nolan, and Conor, the jury was considering dropping the charges. Sophie and Conor testified that she was only doing what she thought was right because of her illness. But Nolan, being the one who was shot, had the choice of whether to press charges on Ms. Lana. Nolan decided not to press charges but was quickly overruled by his parents who pressed charges against her citing "parental fury." So after two weeks of debating among the jurors, they concluded that Lana was found not guilty due to insanity. The judge sentenced Lana to spend 3 months in a mental health facility with an additional 6 months on house arrest.

Lastly, it was time for Ms. Struss to face trial for the involuntary manslaughter of Belle Frank. This gathered attention across the city, with hundreds of people showing up in support of Ms. Struss. At the trial, Sophie and many other people testified for Ms. Struss in support. It was a lengthy trial, lasting over a week before coming to a decision.

The jury foreman stood up and announced "Your honor, we the jury have found Trista Struss guilty..."

The courtroom went into shock but was quickly silenced by the judge.

"...of trespassing on private property but is found not guilty of involuntary manslaughter.

The courtroom went into cheers and applause in light of the news.

"Silence!" yelled Judge Jarid. "Ms. Trista Struss."

"Yes, your honor?" said Ms. Struss

"You are a very lucky lady and never in my 30 years of being a judge has witnessed such a case like yours. But as for trespassing, I have decided to sentence you to pay a $10 fine. Case dismissed."

The judge slammed his gravel which signified the end of this case.

Sophie and Ms. Struss hugged very tightly.

Two weeks later after the trial, Sophie's life has changed for the better. To commemorate the start of a new chapter in her life Sophie has gotten a haircut. Walking into school, Sophie was greeted by many people who she can call friends now. She walked into the cafeteria where she saw Conor and Jimmy.

"Hi nerds!" said Sophie.

"Hey Sophie!" said Jimmy.

"Hi Sophie, did you get a haircut?" asked Conor.

"Yes, thanks for noticing," said Sophie. "So what y'all been up to?" she asked.

"I have been working on my art," said Jimmy.

"Nothing much for me," said Conor.

"Hey loser."

Sophie turned around to see Tia and her group standing right behind her.

"You might be popular as me, but don't forget who saved Nolan," said Tia before walking off.

After the trial, seeing how popular Sophie was, Tia kept reminding people of Nolan's rescue to keep some attention to herself to no avail.

"Ready for our plans, tonight?"

Albert Cooper III

Sophie turned around to see Nolan coming towards her.

"Of course I didn't forget," said Sophie.

Later that day, at an ice cream shop, Sophie and Nolan were conversating while waiting for their food.

"I honestly can't believe this all happened.' said Sophie.

"Same, it's like it's straight out of a book," said Nolan.

"Hey, but I'm glad it happened cause we wouldn't be getting ice cream if not," said Sophie.

"But still, a couple of sophomores solving a mystery that even the police couldn't solve. It kinda makes our police look incompetent," said Nolan.

"You really need to stop overthinking stuff," said Sophie.

"How many times are you gonna say that?" asked Nolan.

"As many times as I need to," said Sophie.

"Aww, how romantic," said Ms. Struss walking by their table.

"We're just friends, Mom," said Sophie. "Hold up, what are you doing here?"

"Honey, did you forget I've been working here for a week? replied Ms. Struss. "Also, I don't want any grandchildren yet so if you and Nolan have plans tonight, do it at his house."

"MOM!!!"

THE END

ABOUT THE AUTHOR

Albert Cooper III is a Georgia native, raised in a small town. An avid literary reader, he often imagines writing a book of his own. So that is what he did! Before shifting into writing full-time while in college, he was either playing his trumpet, walking around his neighborhood, or playing with his cat and dog.

Made in the USA
Columbia, SC
15 October 2022

69513999R00046